TWISTED TONGUE

ALSO BY SUALIMON OLAJIDE KWAM

Peace: A panacea to Nation Building

The Signal: Accomplishing Personal Establishment

Beautiful Things: Poem Compilation

For more information on his books
You can email to instincthillincorporated@gmail.com

Foreword

Poetry is the art of expression with words in unique form. The pattern at which words are use in narration of event or thoughts in distinctive ways air the ability of proper articulation of feelings in benefitting ways suitable to the poet.

Twisted Tongue is another poem compilation by Sulaimon Olajide Kwam. A compilation enriched with impactful contents and knowledge encompassing aimed purposeful living and getting along with life challenges.

This is beyond poem compilation, it serves as word artistry to guide people on living right and just, adapting to life and challenges, overcoming difficulties and round enhancing a fulfilled life.

Twisted Tongue is knowledge orientated, depicting life encounters in all ramification, indicating process and pattern by which basis for daily situation can be handled and scaled.

Sulaimon Olajide Kwam

Instincthill Incorporated

Preface

This compilation of poems is more of expression of love and getting along with life with affection in midst of increase complexity on circumstances pertaining to living. It is obvious worlds problem is now compounds adding to demands of not just living but getting along on full of challenges. Twisted Tongue is a taste of poetry narrating conditions attached to modern time life and also indicating measures and pattern by which we can get by with the moment of time to have an untroubled period and smooth running at occurrence life wavering situation.

~ Sulaimon Olajide Kwam

SUBTLETY

World is adrift

Planets immersed in distance

Universe revamped to human's style

Mother earth in parts of pattern of races

Each depicts levels of advancement

In its parts, its inventions

Mans' products as it were

Always attached with price.

Beauty lost when tapped

Beauty formed from pretty hands

Planets made to transformed in makings

Masterpiece established as conceived

In pattern that pleases

We have the world made by hands.

Complexity of world compounds

Intense situations get

Tentacles broaden in scope

Beyond steers to direct to appeal path it seems

Uniformity lost at directional

Clenches of races to grasps

Pedaled to paths of wishes.

Comfort from ease is aftermath of discoveries

By modernization it's earned

Complicated is denial of fact

Obvious but repulsive for not appealing

Tracks lost from anew trends

Reshaped to pattern of events.

Subtlety.. Subtlety…

Pace should bridge

Races interwoven with conceptualization

Destination abounds by time

Uncertainty in hasten pace

Slowly should we veer

Mindful for what's put to world

Preservation of world's beauty

Should benchmark mans' interest.

MOUNTAINS IN THE SKY

Erected in positions its spotted

Firmly sharp of forms in sizes

Tall, average, medium in same makes

Above ground it holds flag

Upon floors its beyond

Suffices atop are floors beneath

Surfaces not at par from sight.

Climb atop and stare below

Same floors suffice another beneath

Hips crimpled in forms to height

Unfathomed to sharping of place

To sky it climbs up

Ascends to peak can attained

Like stairs taking to cloud formed in prints

Exhausted it stopped by height of mountain.

Mountains above the ground

Some sighted in heights

Others beyond sight can spotted

Reduced to spot by hovering of clouds

Choses to level up than be at par to floors

Undisturbed its choses from troubles of being

Hell of trouble it'll cost to reach its top.

Spot a mountain above the cloud

Lovely and tempting to reach

Before you embark for cruise of adventure

Akin it to Everest

You may never get halfway or even close

Eventually if you take on the adventure

May as well be walking in cloud and above

Sighting amazing clouds forms mountains in the sky.

EITHER WAYS

Strong is feelings

Compunction for interest

Gleaming of captivations

Attractions to attributes

Attachments to attitude

Choices made on qualities.

Desires grows

Options sprouts

Choices narrows

Blazingly to path

Upon which if veered

Desires could be ours.

Thinking is starting point

Many things it birthed

Desires to choices

Choices to actions

Paths adequately established

Determination key to accomplishment.

Success is multifaced

No ways are either way

Well defined and thoughts through

By thoughts we attune to making

In ways of choices

Be rightly placed to act

At roles of desires.

QUENCH THE FLAMES

Frequent trial of feelings shaded by love

Taught to heart the significance to feel

Teachings never levels

Differ scale of love is developed through living

We live in measures of love

With cares shown from onset of life.

Love is flames that continually burns in heart

Unshown and awaiting ignition

To showcase what's long concealed by heart

From offspring of love to maturation

Love and be loved in return

For that whom care is given.

When flames burn in heart

Perhaps for whom is loved

Tendency may not reciprocate on scale

Hearts' not seen but felt

By feelings love strutted

When heart burns emotions erupt.

Love ought tally

Equation of feelings it conveys

Variation when scale surpasses one

Something's amiss that's unknown to second

Plain and unmanipulated love is

It burns in sincerity

Reflection of feelings by means

One-sided noticed at decline

Insinuate flames of love about to quench

From the very heart that loves at first.

TABLE OF MEN

Have thy seat not with clenched thoughts

If thou would sit amidst men

Circumference of values should gauge

Thy worth measures by orchestration

Caliber of men classified in gathering

In qualities alike

In thoughts identical.

Be with folks as thou be seen

No words of you would be said by thee

Your clicks thy world

Words spoken in attributes

Men in green are likes of makes

Bangles of values they're bond

Togetherness stands for what they stood.

Your seat reserved at table of men

Take rightful place of where you should

Men of actions and character seated affront each

Neither intimidated nor scared by appearances

Integrity is centerpiece of event

Utmostly upheld to life as breath

Their words not let lose

Until necessary to heard

Having spoken, it weighs profundity.

THE HANDSHAKE

In heads are worlds

Worlds of chosen and makings

From present to future

Lives attuned to abstract

Which we craved to lived

In that we make from life.

Ideas turns to dreams as yields

Collectively proceed to makings

In gradual at stages

Personified we become

In ways best to attain

That the dreams entail.

Bodily, we guzzled

Qualities of world afar

Steps to connection of ideas

World of ideas we yen

Beseeming as progress

Apts with time.

Time is endless

Dreams are myriad

Choice is splay

Effort is willful

Achievement is prolificity

The makings of man they are.

End points of wants

Longing of past in present day

Transposed we are to world

Connection to making of self

Brain and mind sync

Glad to find in position

Bodily slants welcomed by world

Liked minds to handshakes

Positions pleasant to contained.

WHERE IS YOURSELF

Where is yourself

Appraise at obvious when no longer self

Grandeur of yesterday lost

Heritage repressed

Dishevelment of people in purlieus

At guidance they ought be directed

In motif brought by old.

Missed are things you stood

Prowess of custom held high of yesterday

Much respect attributed by which they led

Footprints left behind to be followed

Instead to step on same prints of foots

Foots takes different paths of prints

Deviation to accustomed

People turns aliens to themselves.

Missed ways to recreation of type

That which you stood should've been sustained

Before you, were your kinds

At your feet impresa of labor laid

How come today is inversely

When labor of yesterday tends not to yield

And radiate in kinds of today.

Where is yourself

Today is different from how it should

Otherwise are situation cuz you're mixed

Diluted liquids changes color

So those values altered interwoven at balance

If limit not streamline

Path for what you stood are missed.

TIDY SOUL

Serenity... undisputed calmness of surfaces

Interrupted by influence of beings

Existence have brought much damage than repair

Thinking, the essence of life

Spring to stance of things

Upon which world is conditioned.

Madness, product of thoughts

Craziness, product of madness

Transmissible by impacts

Refinement of behavior

Transcends to actions in vicinage

Conformity in reactions by people.

Never will you be in places forever

Life nature is by nature of earth

Rotational we move around in globe

Certainty in midst of strangers is guaranteed

Baffled not should you be

If reactions malign that of yours.

Ideally, it's right to learn anew what's cognized

Nothing is done in way but multiple

What's learnt in places could better off kenned

Against your nature could also serve at times

Ideologies lard thinking

Coaxing reaction contrary to normalcy

Straining intellectual functioning to adapt

Disparity in reaction varies by musing

Keeping a tidy soul

Requires little but to stay away from crowd

Sanity attained in serenity of soul.

FLOW WITH BLOOD

Veins will not last forever

As it housed by body

Blood runs to sustain moments

Let it flow till the last wink

In tiny lining in whole

Extended to bloods of blood.

Generations cedes to moments

Home is house dreams lives

In absence still felt

Dreams continues at life's farther

Cuz blood runs in same vein

That runs as same in yours.

In your dealing with makes

Look through eyes with dreams

It's being lived with avenues

Make it flow in their veins

Dreams is in home

Let it flow with blood.

STAMPEDE

Swallow not tomorrow in horror of present

For the present reserved for future

If act in haste to have tomorrow in present

Present could be choked by what future possessed

Lavished would be at moment

When it could be sustained for future.

What lies in earthily world

Is enough for universe

Oceans remains, never drained at once

By little, we fetch needs to quench taste

Scooping from shores by large

To brim, oceans remain in stillness.

Water, a source never planted

Nor prodded to surge

Naturally flows by indiscernible means

Distinguished in uniqueness by nature of earth

Same, are not of others

Reach of man, are decisive to sources of nature.

Fruits unreplaced when plucked

Left to rot when dumped

Periodical its aback when given time

On plants that serve purpose with numbers

Reach of sources tally the people

Germane are soils for products of plants

On surface its tent is structured.

Speed is needless to hastiness to time

Consumption is by figures of needs

By people, needs quantified

By products, needs compresses

Compartment to soil and people

Overwhelmed it get when population is outstretched.

HELD FROM BEHIND

Grounds not in fused parallel

Acquaintance with paths never bespeak perfection

Mastery to veer by guides of heart

With sights we stick to steps

Even when paths are well used

We still miss steps and at times falls

Not by how we mis-stepped

But by what sights missed when we stepped.

Falling not outlandish

Steadily it happens

Persistence in getting back up in multiples

Fall and stand and walk again

It keeps going on in recurrence

Lucky you are for stretched hand

Hooked to pull up by someone close.

Disdain is art of man

Relinquished to despair of qualities

Greatest falls are not by mis-steps

Loathing and scorn have pulled down than ever

Held by hands from behind

Forethoughts of falling behind is foreseen.

When taken aback in cause of destiny

One thing certainly leads to another

Feats happens not as envisioned

Kismet takes steers and gears

In midst of people, you'll be held

Straight to where you ought to be.

FIELD OF ROSES

Garden of roses allures in beauty

Cultivation adored with aloofness

Enticement seen at close

Touch asserts reflection of heart for affection

Feelings depicted in beauty

Roundish shape of feelings of emotions.

Connecting to warmth of mind

Field of roses akin of flowers

One at hand coequal in ground

Same beauty upheld

Only choice is of sizes

To nurture or go for fading beauty.

Beauty is in eyes beholder

Roses are not in ladies' form

Reflection of beauty it depicts in looks

Image conferred what the heart feels

But ladies and roses are two variables

Object of beauty

Subject of nature.

Nature, binding of kinds

Fixed to purpose of existence

Accepted for that it is best known

By which we tend to appreciate

What it stands for.

Ladies takes form of nature

Titillating beauty in different shape

Certainty of roses fixed to appreciation

Ways of ladies, field of genteel

Posture not precise by guise or beauty

Roses of humans is innate

By attitude and attributes, it's expressed

Adorned by values it presents.

DIVE TO THE AIR

Hecticness has no bounds

Brains has its limit

Capacities are infinite

By strength its absorbed

Strong grabs what it can

To withstand wavering moments of life

Shades or light, it throws one into

Strong or weak, we get refined.

Get set and be ready

Future is challenge however seen

Toss of self to thee

Awaiting in that for which we craved

Beware of its demands

A dive to the air you could be taking

Gravity is lost cause

Afloat in air is loss of control.

Astronauts are not in free will

To case of that of earth

Nor divers in oceans breath beneath

Air excepted at both

Filled to brim ocean is

Free to space gravity is

Either gravity or ocean

Be ready to set sail

And get along with what's needed.

Before you take a step

Or alter a path

Cognize that which you need know

Entente is diving to lost in directions

To be made

Or marred by ignorance.

IN MOMENT OF TRUNCE

Spare fling in might of strength

As though the last spare of life

Aimed for another day to be seen

Destruction to living that stand in ways of living

Two cannot live on purpose of importance

Strike is aftermath to eliminate hindrance to purpose.

Havoc to half is none at all

Taken out completely secures the aim

To have whole to oneself

Autonomy is absolute authority

Urge never ending

The causes of feuds.

It takes two to tangle

More for feuds

Infinite peace precedes freedom

Will to have in control things at reach

To put at scale of this in place

Two must come in contact in ways to garb.

Desires burns dearest like wildfire

Sweeping across trees spreading

So.., the heart burns for that it loves

Not willing to let go in midst of interests

Matured is mind calm to threat of interests

Instead of destruction and violence

To kill or harm

Compromise we arrived to avoid feuds.

THROUGH THE HEART

Shut the eyes

Summon the soul

Sealed in dolls

Thereof no breath

Nor existence worthwhile

Therein the body

Lies the soul in heart.

Soul is at cruise

Adventure to life

Living is beyond world

Departed soul upheld memories

Worldly part to spiritual realms

Souls never extinct

Eternity, it exists.

By the heart,

Lives forms…

By the heart,

We live…

By the heart,

We tell our story…

Through the heart,

We make meaning out of us…

DROWNING LOVE

Don't be scared to give it all

Give it when time is right to explore

Feelings is for he who cares

Caring is to be shown of love

Thrown into what is believed

Soaked as marinated in-love

Expression of what is felt is shown.

Believe is to trust

Trust is to be entrusted upon

For that we thought it deserved

Relentless we are to give part of us away

Set to drown we throw thee

Attached emotion is risk taken

Half of us placed on line of risk to lose.

Be careful and not carefree

Be timely and aware

Be truthful to emotions

Not senseless to expression

Love is façade of feelings

Act of loving in attitude

Hidden in truth that truly cares.

Drowning love is mistaken

From onset interest swallowed

Amazing how feelings are shrouded

Pretentious by nature are beings

Deceitful should not be left out of equation

To ruin it may lead one

When the whole is put into love.

YESTERDAY'S FORGOTTEN

Oh! I exclaimed to thy

If thou knoweth what today would

Perhaps, different it would as it turns in pages

That flips in progress of comprehension

To read till last end of book.

Yesterday in history

Occurrence of events in lifetime

Before and during lifespan

Of diaries of life lives

In ages past in time

But certainty is recurrence

As time tics in same figures.

Nothing anew in existence

Today will as well pass to ages

Later termed as yesterday to be remembered

Or forgotten by its irrelevance

And hold place in history

For that, that once occurred.

Upon we live to time maturation

Cognizance of past and present

Shaping today's direction from yesterday

Not to be wanting in yesterday's event

So, we seek that which is amiss

Forgotten about yesterday to be of known

As time ticks to tomorrow

Perfection we craved in life events.

Dig within and around

Dig to what makes histories

Found therein wrongs and rights

Against or favored they were at moments

Forgotten they tends,

If moment is not befitting

And little value to thee.

TOMORROWS' DIARY

Tomorrow's far but near

Hours just away to unfolds

Minute is gift, hours a present

Treasure of breath opportune to have

Found in today as tomorrow approached

The day next to another

Written to records as it comes.

Diaries made hands of days

Pagess filled with one's written of yesterday

Upon which they were tomorrows'

In hands of time

They made their time

Sequel to series of days and years

Diary of years made by days.

Tomorrow's diary takes off from yesterday

Existence is sequential events

Only approached in moment of time

State of will in future

Narrowing in specific direction

To will of future wanted written in diary.

TWISTED TONGUE

Entangled emotions drown

Compassion marinates to empathy

Twisted blues forms of feelings

Souls mingling in passion

Words not enough for what's felt

Speechless not silence

With gaze fixated to eyeballs

Says all needed to know.

Words loses values at expense of feelings

Arouse in presence of love, be calm…

Language best understood is close proximity

Hold and be held

Feel softness of touches caresses the body

Souls lightened as goosebumps swells on skins

Lost in love, lost in souls.

Lips couldn't speak

Words are far away and couldn't be reached

Breaths in constant seizure anticipating to aligns

Lips lost and tongues glued to jaws

At close range, expression falls to rhymes

Heads moves a closed, nose sideways to each

Lips locked at kiss

Twisted tongues at deep

Love conveyed without words

Two lovebirds drown in souls of feelings.

IN FACE OF TRUTH

Face tells it all

We need not speak

Intents seen in looks

Even if word alters otherwise

Expression before we speak

States the state of mind.

Truth maybe hidden in words

Fickle are words in values

Measures are in person

You weigh the impact of words

If it stands what's altered

Your measures of words plinth for truth.

Let thy face be repute

Frequented by validity

This, you'll be kenned for what's said

Fact to face by words

Appealing to be seen always

Genuity of thy heart

Present face for truth

Always ready to be listened

When words are altered.

GROUND ZERO

Hills of life never at peak

Everest above mountains is beneath the sky

Conditions attached to position at levels

Each by efforts of wants

Becoming that once envisaged

In making of self in future

Starting point took place way aback.

Midway to life

Intermediary placed at interface

Interval by points proceed to end that started in past

Phase by phase

We attain in bits

Positions in gradual move.

Desires never ease with flames

Nor dreams seize for future

Positions are decisive to sustain

Making of life is by comfort of man

Aspiration has its want

For its yields, we must oblige.

Ready to set-off

We prepare the mind

Risk stationed in ways taken

Withstand and bear what stands in ways

For aims are not always at ease to attain

Hurdles we embark upon to take when mind is made.

Ground zero

The level we take-off

Putting all we own in line

Not minding how it veers

Journey is on, no going back

Till we get close to where we want

On ground we maybe that of wish.

NO MATTER THE DISTANCE

Close to you

That's where I'll always be

Even if we're thousands of miles apart

Minds connected as though signals transmitted

Ways never too far by distance apart

Nor farther for you to be reached

Feelings will always find means to connect

To feel what has long been felt for whom is loved.

No matter the distance

What we'd would always be held high

Bond shared inseparable by paths

Perhaps what we need to be stronger

Distance to make up for what we lack

Home sweet home calls

In our paths, alone we are

As we work our parts to having home

We realized we're close to getting home.

UNFOLD THE FUTURE

Tomorrow leftover of today

Today hangover of yesterday

Yesterday mystery of days past

Past aftermath of events

Foretold to the future

Of what will be of tomorrow.

The future start from now

From what's made from past

Unravels are event of future

By act of man, it's told

Through activities of now

Future present itself at hand.

Future is untapped

In the mind, it resides

Through acts, it unfolds

By form of what's conceived

Gradually we find ways to that we craved

Directing mind to act in accordance to it.

Unfold the future

Tell your story by living

Live in accordance to dreams

Act in accordance to dreams

Find ways by steps to future

Unfold the life you want to live therein.

WAIT BY THE DOOR

Hanging on little longer

Waiting a little longer

Stopping a little longer

To think a bit longer

For appropriation to situation

Could be best for what to do in haste.

You, a product of thoughts and actions

Present, proceeds of responses

Future, outcomes from situations

All in lieu to efforts

In itself beyond strength and striving

Well served when perseverance applied

In spheres of circumstances.

At times you feel stepping out the door

At times into the door

When situations prompt response

If meant with exact expectation

In hands of events, we ride

We align to it as happened.

When we wait when prompted to act

Stopped when prompted to walk away

Seize lips to alter words in time of desperation

A lot of things we could be prevent

Troubling is aftermath of misdeeds and action

Its elimination validated through moment of seize

Ponder and deliberate in thinking before responding

Actions returns back in multiple ways.

DEEM THE LIGHT

Darkness looms

In facet of glooming day

At all angles

Odds of fortunes

Hidden in acts of man

Clouds brightness in facet of things

Fades light of effort of man.

We strive in fate

Committed to struggles

Believing and hoping

That effort will payoff

But things do not always turn as thoughts

For action of men is beyond man.

Obvious is aftermath of reaction

By scale of effort outcome becomes

Connected always we are to people

Impact in ways as we relate

In attitudes attunes events

By determination situation whirls

Favorable to aspiration

Even though it takes long to accomplishment.

Shine though in parts of world

Even and odds dwells thereabout

Prosperity is even

As odds signals misfortunes

Deem thy light

Sparkled thoughts meet reactions

Even if odd comes from reactions of man

It got shrugged away and never matters.

BROKEN TRUTH

Shouldered are lies hidden in words

Words are true for what they stand

Combined are what it expresses

Impression speaks best at byword

Composure as words drops gauges

Truth, intention of deeds

Spoken in words in exact act

Reflect pose it's altered.

Act in lieu to deeds matching thinking

Very essence of deeds

Reaction should neither overcloud deeds

Nor emphasized on done acts

Let's truth be unbroken

Deeds unfalsified and undenied.

Hoax not for what's not done

Deny not for what's done

For truth stand for what it is

Unbroken by facts

Clinked to worth of esteem

The repute of character.

Be for what you are

Be for what you stand

Be for that you repute

Conceived you are by word of words

Misconstrued you get when words are otherwise

Broken truth never gets fixed

Fixed, it is to your repute.

HELD BY SHOULDER

Despair, avant-garde it portends

Assuage when necessary

By those that ignite

For that best savvied

Against the will of interest, they're kenned

Diminished is aim to demoralized what's aimed.

Denial is constant for optimist

Aftermath of wish perceived by pessimist

Judgement is what's right and just

Rebuffed by low minds that belittle interest

Hallow in fear in prospect of stake

Little minds in despair of great dreams.

Dreams actualized is beyond mind

Ups and downs are common

Dreams dreamt are held high

Togetherness is attained

When held on shoulder with likes

Everything'll be eased.

A hand on shoulder

In moment of toughness

Could be touch needed feel

To tell that support is rendered

Even when the face is unseen

We fathomed that someone cares.

THE PRICE

Vision fruit of thoughts

Dreams fruits of vision

Efforts seeds of dreams

Events paths to dreams

Circumstances price for dreams

Situations combination of all.

Thoughts comes with vision for future

Dreams comes with price

When vision is gazed upon

Know the price to pay

For it lays paths to events

That actualized dreams had.

Price for life is living to future

Price for future is getting along with situations

Laid by dreams as they were

Attainment is fruits of seeds sow

Grown by present with situations suiting dreams

Living in moment with price paid.

SITTING ON ICE

Places are permanent

Infinite use for souls in lifetime

Same terrain different lives

Modified to taste of moments

Different time, different pattern

Modernization absolute by transient.

Souls are temporal

Every breath will be halted

Moments are in nature of soul

In time of being memories established

Held by what it'd at period

Left behind for those beyond.

Life is timely by ages

Moment pace and time flies

Ages transcends with stages

Periodical it's scaled

No stage takes much of time

Ascends by age and stages

Moment pass-by in life.

Nothing last forever

Stages are temporary

Certainty of aftermath is sure

Future ditto to positions

Infinity not guaranteed

Icing of thoughts

We seat on establishment of past.

SEIZE THE MOMENT

Hereafter is far but close

Hours away may never see light for another

Endless are days to come

Anticipation of its expectation

Patiently awaiting its qualities therein

Relentlessly striving to have it at hand

Like nature that takes moment to effect

We seize the moment as we await.

Never let time passes

For goodies of moment lies thereof

When gone, never retrieve

Moment closes to morrow

Today maybe far from offing

Amidst distances apart

While apart, seize the moment.

Things doesn't just happen, know that

Ennobling inures everything itched

Await moment to come through to have that

Don't just wait, make use of moment

If instant scaled without utility

May never be found again

That you aim to have in moments

May seize to come

For the past was wasted.

ROLL THE DICE

Success!!! Game of factors

Have balls at hand and roll on palm

Make it spring at edges

At times it falls why you pick back up

On and on it lingers

Till you decide to halt

And drop ball at will.

Game of factors

Marvels in shape of events

Trend paths you stare

Scenes happens with steps

Like dices rolls in hands

Thrown to ground

Figures shown at still.

Events comes

Scene happens

We roll like balls on ground

Dices to scene with action

Reaction totems to events

Afterwards it's figures present.

Roll the dices

Game of factors appears like figures

Appealing or not

Wheel held with hands

Decide where to steer

Directions are yours to take.

LET IT RAIN

Calmness, Calmness., the essence of society

Sane are people therein

Serenity impacted by untroubled spirit

In all is found by what they stood

To maintain its sanity

Or have it lost to chaos

Left to people for society's' making.

When hell is let loose

Serenity lost

Insanity status quo of normalcy

People loses core essence of society

Strangers to their own makes

Aliens to their world

Deviation from lands' norms

Earth seems to be against them

Then hell is let loose with unrest.

When it radiates

Trembling of soil as though landslide to occur

Everywhere hot as if celsius at peak

All they need do is look upon the sky

Summons the clouds to set for rain

Watch closely as it becomes fluffy in darks

Stand beneath if it drizzles

Patiently withstand its downpour

To cleanse the untroubled spirit of the soul

And make them anew afresh

For sanity to return back its sphere.

POINTLESS

Rather late than not

Reckon with shortfalls as fault of character

Stress not misdeed of actions

Imperfection in art of living

Flaws prone to behaviors

Condemn not that not appealing

Different ways of reactions we are.

Acknowledge that processions differ

Molding ignites behaviors

Reactions prompted by patterns of understanding

As variety of thoughts varies to single thing

No one is expected to think as same as another

Or respond to expectations of fellows

For climes of thoughts are by tent.

Antagonize when necessary

Condemn no aim but to correct

Virtues of character not always certain

Prone we are to flaws of imperfection

Decisive is reactions on pattern to respond

Considerate we get as we justify.

Overhitting on wrongs is pointless

Needless be distracted for what's gone haywire

Criticism of faults diminishes morale

Stigmatized not for what went wrong

Bounds is nature by mistake

Common to thoughts of reactions.

SATISFACTORY MIND

Period of needs arises

Longings and desires above reach

At immediate we lack what it takes to address

Beyond windows of hands, we take hand

Barriers to needs not out of reach

By capacities we seek whom is fit to render

That very thing craved badly to have.

Doubts arises in moments of leanings

Wants only known to persons by importance

Little relevance to whom willing to render

Two things come to mind of person in hands of needs

Significance to whom in wants

Benefits to whom in hands

Mind interject to take roles of kinds

If necessary to put person above whom in needs.

Interjectory of benefits to whom in hands

Takes tow on positions and pattern to renders

Attached to conditions are seeking minds

Exploring circumstances to scale of needs

One at hand one in possession

Give and take scenario to balance longings

Bait of hands, bait to wants

Conditions attached to shown

Left for acceptance or to forgo

For whom in needs or seek alternate.

Plain-hearted never weighs importance to self

Consideration of impact it prioritized

Without much ado needs to wants gratified

Hands thrown open to needs

Not placing one above other

When obvious one's ahead of other

Even in moment of unmeant needs.

HOSTILE ARENA

Establishment without foresightedness

Purpose without aim

Goal without objective

Dreams without vision

Desires without direction

Existence without nurturing

Floppy the clay is in settings.

Beings without attributes

Futile it is in values

Worth of arena measured by its structure

Therewith housed it assets

Concern not about the arena

Concern more about the beings.

Nature remains plain in context

Defined by its content

Beings its contemporaries

Key aspects of its components

Refined it get with capabilities

In taste of civility.

Civility is expensive

Purchased by procedures

Pattern sated in beings' acceptance

Thereof slated expressions

Perception conceived in vicinity

Arena it's meant to sheer.

Hostile arena

Not much to say

But much to heard

A lot to cheer

Celebration of nags

Making bad out from good

And ugly from bad

For no just reason

Justified as nurtured.

RING OF LIES

Actions are seed of deeds

Opinions' products of thoughts

Perspective, processing of thinking

Comprehension aftermath of processing

Perpetual is behaviors

Perception inculcated by thinking.

Faculty is complex

Diverse in immensity

Timid is thinking

Dreaded for its difficulty

Task of life of thinking

We embark on training to enhance.

Ring of thoughts we conformed

Layer of perspective formed

Fine tune to basis of opinion

For cognitive to be sound

Words matches thoughts

Opinions matches thinking.

Ring of thoughts conforms

Ring of conformity, accepts

What is thrown out is left to open

To determine genuity of opinion

Truth remains what it stands

Lies thrown from lips of thoughtlessness

Never weighs impact of what's said

Nor consequence of opinion formed.

Filter the bangle of words

Know the lips its' spoken

Ring of truth, and

Ring of lies are same

Making of thoughts

Shaping of perception

Opinions formed by both.

UNWAVERING LOVE

Flexibility of heart timid minds to love

At slightest sight for whom it's felt

Hesitation shove even at reluctant

Doubts toss to wind as though doesn't matter

Even if aftermath of outcome perceived

Of how heartbroken we might get at end

We seize to care at instance

For what matters is love we feel.

Love blends, paraded in discomfort

Mending of souls becoming one

Tribulation becomes strength

Stronger are bonds that binds feelings

Banes of emotions outstretched to love

Unhindered by pulls of emotions from one's love

Unwavering love upheld by heart that's prepared for it.

FLOATING CANDLE

Watch day gloom in gold at sunset

Radiance of full sun at gaze to set

Harsh of heat reduces for calm

Setting, paving ways as dark looms

Blending into opposite clouds from rise

Lightening to golden as it fades to night.

Numb the sky get at first

Darkest looms in wee hours of day

Unnoticed in appearance

Glaring is day as night approaches

Though spotted at distance in time

Awaiting moment to gloom the darkest.

Shades falls upon as lightening took off by sun

Night set in and reveal that universe is dark

Illumination of night with little light is not by moon

Without sun in far radiance to its distance

Another planet be termed with little relevance

But by its significance, it is upheld

The floating candle, illuminating the night.

SHAPING DESTINY

Mind, means of channeling pattern

Resolute by person

Means to getting along

From past to present to future

Paths trends on precepts

Destiny shaped by process.

Ways to future is complex

In making, we classified

In phases, we shape into that

By hands of making

Adapting to demands

We create the future

Shaping our destiny.

Destiny is challenges

To live in one's making

Through difficulties it brought forth

Process person into that

For which it wishes to become

At moment when it's right.

LOST FRIENDS

Today will be for today

Known for what went therein

Nothing is for eternity

Despite frequency of tics

Moments falls to past

Riddled of yesterday

Lost moment of days.

Days get along with people

Dearest to heart we bear

Love for what they are

We share in bodies in souls

Two bodies in a mind

Friendship distinct on what's shared.

Friendship last forever, people say

But just words altered

Beyond that a lot goes in

Love shared tested if to bonds

Long to hold if test pass

Friendship remains when weighed

Dearly, we see each as beloved.

Best of friends at times haven't seen it all

Slightest of things could strain its strength

Qualities of bonds pulled at stretch

By differences we conceived what persons are

Inset by reactions

Triggered we get

Friendship could be lost

If well not behaved.

HANDS LET LOSE

Tightly cliched fiercely to fist

Grabbing closely to that difficult to lose

As though whole is hinged

Not ready to go

Burden to heart for dear to life

We keep holding as though we'll die when lost.

Treasures not discovered until mined

Gold barely shaped until heated to form

Hands merely useful until put to use

Gifted it turns when discovered to best

Loose is fist when grabs is let lose

Lost cannot be replaced without lose

Better comes for what's lost

We've been used to it anyway.

Fear set in for we know not what to come thereof

Mindset activated to lookout for worst

Like stone held to shore of sea

Hands freed to let lose as we see drop to bed

Sitting beneath, untroubled by its waves

Settled we attunes when fear to lose get eventually lost.

Hands clinched fiercely is tight fisted

Never free for anything till opened

Enclosed it is to grabs

Struggle we keep on when clinched

That held is already part of

Nothing anew to be added

If not drop what's else

Hands cannot be free to receive.

DYING SOUL

Captured from birth mystery of body

Bore at hand display of soul

Reality set with fact of death

Befalling upon to depart in time

While moments extend to its period

We seize to enjoy the moment.

Daily dying to grave

Close and close it gets near

Moments counts to years

Periodically at interval we depart

Souls leaves the body

At when it's willed.

Dying soul

Consumed with thought of it but unbothered

Health is good so we think it's all fine

Afflicted with ailments we know we are close

Health declines we know death approaches

Life drains away from bodily deterioration

Indicating fading soul set to die.

HATRED AND LOVE

Feelings are lightening propelled to brightens

Positioning of source to certain direction

Fixed of bulb to its surrounding

At will, turned on and off at needs

So is nature of life

To love and to hate.

When you love you feel

When you hate you feel

Same energy propelled by one source

Ability to feel and express emotions

Ironically, baffling to know that hatred is feelings

Likewise, as love.

Hatred and love

Same source from the heart

Feelings are channels of emotions

Expression to pattern of thinking

Constantly in control of feelings

Despair, hatred, and love

All choice of feelings

Straight from heart

We decide what to feeling subsequently.

THE BLUE MOON

Day is setting off

Weariness weld in from strenuousness

Blurry thoughts get as thinking becomes feeble

Actions turns doodle at sunset

Day is called off to rest

Afterglow we set home for recess.

As darkness set in for night

Relaxed we get at comfort of shelter

Indoor maybe tiresome to be

Hecticness compressed by casualty

Change of atmosphere could relief

Outdoor is alternate for calmness.

Take time off as night set in

Under the full moon is best for recess

Glooming the darkness from illuminated sun

Bottle of wine and cigar as companion

Best shared with heart that cares

Talk through the night and listen with love

Weariness will be lost in no mean time

Into the wee hour of night.

TIME AND MONEY

Moments are real

Don't waste it

Nor thrown away to the wind

Blown of ashes into midst of air

Conformed to its likes

Not to be seen as it were.

Know that which is unknown

Know that worthy to be known at moments

Time is money

Time is knowledge

Money is knowledge

Get the knowledge of time

To be at per with time to make money.

Know the difference

Calculate its variance

Correlate between knowledge and money

For the source you crave to earn will reveal

When moment is attained to make money

And time right to earn money.

SPOT THE BEE

Love the produce

know the maker

Taste the produce

Feel the maker

Know the maker

Feel the produce

Interesting of perks attracts to makes

Tastes of pleasure pledged.

Spot the bee

Hover mid air

Somewhere it heads

No farther than beehive

Where colony awaits

To have in midst again.

When you spot the bee

Know its hive is close

Trend softly at sight

Irritated they get with interference

Anger of one trigger colony

For proximity to hive is close.

WORKING IT OUT

Living is hard

Dying is difficult

Life is dreadful

Hurdles its' filled

Pleasantly we harbor closely

As though meaningless the dreadfulness of life is.

Mysteriously the unpleasant becomes pleasant

Solace found in dreadfulness of life

Stillness we are to challenges of world

Undeterred to shortcomings of demands

Unrestrained by effect in getting along

Unbothered to make offspring to witness same.

Events are clinked

In circles it happens as same of past

Experiences partake again in present

New born to become young

Old they get in time

In ways those before lived.

Certainty are circumstances of events

Transfixed are reactions attached

Transient knowledge is

Responses alike if upheld as they are

Quests never ends

Clarity yields more comprehension.

Universe is by what it is

By understanding, meaning is made

Decision is by us to live or deviate

Situations always portrays in two forms

Pleasant or unpleasant

The choice is left

To either work it out

Or live by with what we can make do with what we can.

THE LION'S TAIL

Lion's face consumed with fear who stares

Meanness in jungle it portrays

Death reigns in midst

Absolute to fact it lives

Untimely it appears in forms

Caught up if found

Preys of jungle are all.

Despite being king of hood

Autonomy for prey not limited

Kill and be killed is art of jungle

Rule by which they lived

Animals are all preys

Feed and be fed upon each

Sustenance to eat at raw.

Attribute in hierarchy of attack

Size not by strength

Boldness and skills of attacks placed above other

Appearance in kinds signals capabilities

Each exist as moment permits

Death, the fate of all

Caught up by another with above strength.

Distance from sight

It stands is command of territory

Affront and behind

Is not to get close

It tails still has a say

Even if it cannot roar

That it's still the lions' part.

GOD IS MAN

Perhaps places take course to ascribe meaning

Everything conceived at first are strange

Quest for meaning attributes defines

Every substance beneath clouds identified to items

Each signified to relevance

By importance to nature of attachment.

Creatures are by creation

Existences of species of varies

Marvel is how it takes form

Settings in pattern of perfection

Which cannot be attain by man

On parallel, everything takes form.

Almighty is creator of all

We learnt is God

After God are angels

Powerful, but in abstract They exist

Image of Him man is made

In intellect, could it be same!?

The only distinguish is death

At per man would be

World turns beautiful and damaging by doings

Presumed to be left from where He stopped

What places Him above man

Belief of creation of universe.

Man took off from where he stopped

In its settings of founds

Exploration of universe

Even though natures' deviate to mother earth

Necessities for creatures to exist

Man remakes to its wants

To live therein

From where God stopped.

INESTIMABLE

Risk it

If it worth it

Throw all you have in a cause you believe in

Get your focus on dreams

To level of no turning back

Remain unshakeable

When difficulties come knocking

You'll be just to know not to throw to trash

Dreams fragile like egg

To be handled and nurtured like seed sow to grow

Watered by ideas to germinate

Processed by determination to realized

To come to life as dreamed

Like precious egg hash to life.

Made in the USA
Middletown, DE
13 March 2024